Ernest and Fat Orange Cat

Amy and Philip Rowe
Pictures by
Amy Rowe

Collins

First published 1987 by William Collins Sons & Co Ltd
London and Glasgow
© text Amy and Philip Rowe 1987   © illustrations Amy Rowe 1987

This is a story about Ernest.

Ernest was a mouse.

Ernest was a fierce mouse.

Ernest was fierce every day.

He was fierce on Mondays,
on Tuesdays, on Wednesdays,
on Thursdays, on Fridays,
on Saturdays, on Sundays
and especially on sunny days.

Why especially on sunny days?

Well, Ernest the fierce mouse was
especially fierce on sunny days because
he liked to go for a walk in his beautiful
garden.

Every sunny day morning he got ready
to go out.

But there, in the garden, was a fat,
orange cat.

This fat, orange cat was called Evil.

Evil the cat liked mice.

Evil the cat liked to eat mice for his
breakfast, dinner and tea.

So every sunny day morning Ernest
came out of his hole . . .

. . . and there was that fat, orange cat, Evil.

"Who is that?" said Evil the cat.
"Is that a mouse? I like to eat mice."

He was always very hungry.

Even Ernest the fierce mouse was
frightened,

but he said in a loud voice, "No, I'm not a mouse. I'm an enormous dog with enormous teeth."

"I like to eat cats for my breakfast, dinner and tea.

I eat twenty cats every day. Are you a
cat?" asked Ernest.

Now, of course Evil the cat was
frightened . . .

. . . but he said in a loud voice, "No, I'm not a cat. I'm a lion escaped from the zoo."

"I like to eat dogs for my breakfast,
dinner and tea.

I eat fifty dogs every day. Come out and
I will eat you!'' he roared.

Now, Ernest the fierce mouse was very
brave,

so he went out into the beautiful garden.

But Evil the cat didn't see him.

Evil the cat didn't see him because . . .

he didn't expect to see a mouse.

He expected to see an enormous dog with
enormous teeth.

So Ernest the fierce mouse went for his
sunny day walk.